First published in the UK by HarperCollins Children's Books in 2010

1 3 5 7 9 10 8 6 4 2
ISBN: 978-0-00-735564-8

©SEGA/Sunrise, Nagoya Broadcasting Network.
Dinosaur King is a registered trademark of Sega Corporation. All Rights Reserved.

Written by Matt Crossick

HarperCollins *Children's Books*

WELCOME TO THE WORLD OF DINOSAUR KING!

CONTENTS

DINOSAUR DISCOVERY

It was the middle of the night, and dinosaur-mad Max Taylor was fast asleep in his bedroom, next to his father's dinosaur research lab. Little did he know that his night's sleep was about to be ruined! A huge, fiery meteor was plummeting to earth from space, and it was heading for the forest right next to Max's house. With an enormous crash it ripped through the trees and smashed to the ground, leaving a huge crater in the forest floor.

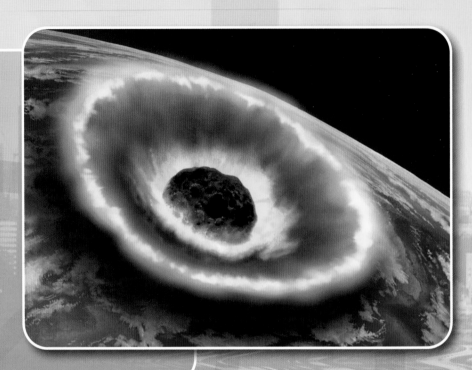

Woken by the meteor tearing through the sky, Max couldn't wait to investigate. He ran down the corridor to wake his friend Rex, called the third member of the D-Team, Zoe, and the three of them rushed into the forest to see if they could find the meteor. Before long, they came across a big area of broken trees and scorched ground – they were definitely getting closer! Next to the clearing, hidden in the shade, there was a battered tree with a large, mysterious hole in the trunk. 'Let's have a look inside!' cried Max. The D-Team was all about adventure, after all!

Nervously, Max reached inside the tree, while Rex and Zoe peered over his shoulder. What could have caused the hole in the trunk? Was it anything to do with the meteor? Scrabbling around in the dark with his hand, Max fumbled across something cold and smooth hidden at the bottom of the hole. As he pulled it into the light, the team saw that it was an ancient-looking stone, with a carving scratched onto it. 'It looks like an electricity symbol, or a lightning bolt!' said Zoe. 'Weird!' said Max. 'What can it mean?'

Rex, meanwhile, was doing some exploring of his own amongst the smashed trees. Lying in the grass, he found a similar stone to the one Max was examining. But instead of a lightning bolt, there was a mysterious swirly wind symbol carved into it. Within moments, Zoe had found a third one – and hers had a grass symbol on it. 'It's like all of the stones have different elements on them!' said Zoe. As the three friends examined their strange finds, Max accidentally flicked the little button underneath his stone. Suddenly, all three stones started to glow brightly, as if they had come to life!

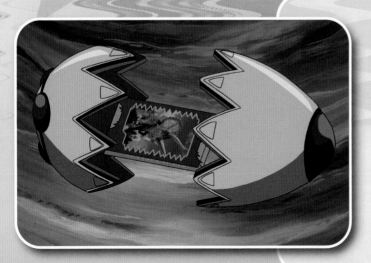

The D-Team gasped. What was going on? The stones must have some magical power, but was it dangerous? All three members looked at each other – they were glowing brightly along with their stones, and a strange noise was coming from the tree with the hole in it. Max carefully approached it and looked inside again. To his surprise, there was an egg in the bottom of the hole that hadn't been there before. It cracked open, revealing two small cards. As the stones stopped glowing, Max reached into the trunk again for a closer look. 'Careful, Max!' cried Zoe. 'There's something weird going on here!'

Max pulled the cards out of the tree, and the D-Team gathered round for a closer look. The cards each had a picture of a dinosaur on them. Max instantly recognised it as a Triceratops – a huge, fierce dinosaur with killer horns. But what had the cards got to do with the strange stones? And why did they suddenly appear like that? Zoe and Rex started looking for more cards in the clearing, but there weren't any to be found...

Max, meanwhile, was sure the cards had something to do with the magic stone. He started pressing them against it, and flicking the switch on the bottom, to see if anything else would happen. As Zoe and Rex gave up the hunt for more cards, Max hit upon the magic formula. He swiped a card along the stone, and it sprung into life, glowing white hot in his hands. 'Guys! Look at this!' he cried. 'Something's happening!' Zoe and Rex rushed over, but froze before they reached Max. An ear-splitting roar ripped through the forest, stopping them dead in their tracks. It came from behind them...and whatever it was, it sounded close!

The three D-Team members gulped. 'Wh-wh-what was that?' stuttered Rex. 'I don't know!' hissed Max. 'But it didn't sound friendly!' The friends turned round slowly as another blood-curdling roar stung their ears. To their horror, a vast, terrifying, real-life dinosaur was rearing up on two legs above them. It was the biggest creature they had ever seen – and it looked angry! 'It's the Triceratops from the card!' cried Max. 'It's come to life!' He turned to Rex and Zoe, but his friends were frozen with fear. Zoe was gazing up at the Triceratops with her mouth open, and Rex was trembling all over.

'B-b-but how?' gasped Max, as the Triceratops slowly lumbered towards the D-Team. 'Dinosaurs died out millions of years ago!' Rex and Zoe edged behind Max and peered out at the massive monster. 'Never mind how!' hissed Zoe. 'You must have brought the card to life with your stone! Now do something to make it go away before it eats us!' But Max was staring up at the dinosaur. 'A real-life Triceratops! Incredible!' he gasped. He couldn't wait to tell his dad about this!

'Max! Snap out of it!' cried Rex, giving him a nudge in the ribs. The Triceratops had broken into a run and was galloping straight towards them. 'Run!' cried Zoe, dashing into the trees. The dinosaur was gaining on them fast, smashing through trees and making the ground shake as it rampaged through the forest. 'Split up!' yelled Rex. 'We need to confuse it!' Max leaped over a log and sprinted as fast as he could. He loved dinosaurs – but that didn't mean he wanted to end up as a dinosaur dinner!

However fast the D-Team ran, they couldn't escape the galloping dinosaur. Rex glanced over his shoulder. 'It's gaining on us!' he cried, stumbling over some bushes. 'Max! Do something!' Out of breath, the three friends ducked behind some trees and watched in horror as the Triceratops roared and smashed its way towards them. 'Like what?' cried Max. 'I don't know how to make it go away!' He pulled the stone out of his pocket and started rubbing and pressing it. 'The card!' cried Zoe, ducking a falling tree. 'Try swiping the card again! And HURRY UP!'

Rex shuddered. They could smell the Triceratops's breath it was so close! Max plunged his hand into his pocket, whipped out the card, and frantically swiped it across the magic stone as they were deafened by another roar. He closed his eyes and waited for the Triceratops to strike...but the blow never came. Instead, he felt a small nibbling sensation in his left leg. 'Wow!' said Zoe as the team slowly opened their eyes again. 'It's gone all cute!' Looking down, Max saw a tiny, yellow Triceratops nibbling at his leg. 'It's transformed!' he gasped, sighing with relief. 'The stone must have shrunk it!'

Their terrifying chase over, Rex and Zoe couldn't help laughing as the tiny Triceratops jumped up at Max and started nibbling him and licking his face. 'He's just like a small puppy – except he's a Triceratops not a dog!' said Rex. 'I think I'll have to call him Chomp!' grunted Max, struggling to escape the dinosaur's tongue. 'He's the cutest dinosaur ever!' laughed Zoe. 'You'll have to keep him as a pet!'

Meanwhile, a huge arena full of people cheered and screamed as a group of dinosaurs ran around in the middle. The arena was bigger than a football stadium, the noise was deafening, and there were dozens of dinosaurs circling and glaring at each other. It was as if they were preparing to fight – and the crowd had paid to watch them rip each other apart!

At one end of the arena, there was a stage with a big throne on it. Here, in the position of honour, sat Dr. Z, surrounded by his Alpha Gang. 'This computer programme shows what my dinosaur arena will be like when it is finished!' he cackled, waving his arm at the cheering crowds and circling dinosaurs. 'All I need is some more dinosaurs to fill it, then I will truly be the DINOSAUR KING!' he carried on, with a manic look in his eye. 'And this arena will be REAL!' 'Yes boss!' sighed Ed, who was sure this would involve some hard work on his part...

With a flicker and a flash, the computer view of the dinosaur arena vanished, and Dr. Z was back in the real world. Dr. Z grimaced as Terry, the only dinosaur he had managed to collect so far, jumped up at him and started nibbling on his beard. 'Get off me, you silly dinosaur!' he grumbled, struggling to break free. 'My beard isn't meant for your dinner! It makes me look good! Now where's the Alpha Gang got to? I have a job for them!'

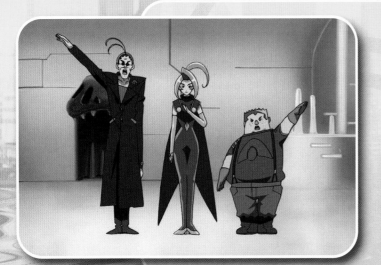

Within minutes, the Alpha Gang were lined up in front of Dr. Z in his hi-tech lab. Zander, Ursula and Ed saluted and waited for instructions from their master. 'As you know,' Dr. Z began, 'I need more dinosaurs for my dinosaur arena. And that means finding more of those dinosaur cards!' The Alpha Gang nodded. 'Yes boss!' they cried. 'Well, a card has been discovered by some children across the world!' Dr. Z cried, rubbing his hands together. 'And I want you to go and get it for me! And don't take no for an answer!'

'Yes boss!' the Alpha Gang cried, and jumped into their custom-made aeroplane to go and steal the card. Of course, Terry went on board with them – they would need a dinosaur to help them with their mission. 'Right, gang! Let's go get ourselves that Triceratops!' cried Ursula as they took off. 'And I don't want you two mucking up the mission this time!' Zander and Ed frowned and nodded. 'Don't worry Ursula!' said Ed, patting the baby Tyrannosaurus. 'No-one can stand up to Terry! Those kids won't know what hit them!'

Meanwhile, back at home, Max's dad Dr. Taylor was puzzling over Max's mysterious stone. 'It certainly looks very old!' he muttered to himself, stroking his beard. 'I've never seen anything like it! And what can that lightning symbol mean?' Max and the others started firing questions at him. 'Where do its powers come from, dad?' he cried. 'How do we control it?' But Dr. Taylor frowned. 'I'll have to examine it in my D-Lab before answering any questions!' he said.

Dr. Taylor was even more amazed when Max showed him Chomp. 'A real Triceratops!' he cried, rubbing his eyes. 'Impossible! How can it be? And why is he so small?' Chomp seemed to sense that he was being talked about – and jumped up to nibble Dr. Taylor's arm! 'Owww!' yelped Dr. Taylor. 'What's he doing?' The D-Team laughed. 'He's called Chomp, dad, and now you can see why!' said Max. 'Can I keep him as a pet?' Dr. Taylor nodded and wrestled Chomp off his arm. 'OK then,' he said. 'But we'll have to tell your mother he's a strange-looking dog!'

But just as Dr. Taylor wriggled free of Chomp, the ground started to shake and a deafening roar blasted over the house. 'That's not a…it couldn't be…' Dr. Taylor gasped. 'It's a real Tyrannosaurus Rex!' The team whirled round to see a giant dinosaur charging towards them. Grabbing a net and a notebook, Dr. Taylor rubbed his eyes and sprinted towards the massive dinosaur. 'Dad! No!' cried Max, and the D-Team shuddered. Surely getting attacked by two dinosaurs on the same day was very bad luck!

The team fled again, the monster-sized Tyrannosaurus Rex shaking the ground as it pounded after them on its huge hind legs. Dr. Taylor abandoned his plans to study the T-Rex and joined the D-Team as they sprinted away from the beast. 'Max! Use Chomp, quick!' cried Zoe. 'We need protection!' Max stumbled as he ran, tripped over a branch, and stared up at the razor-sharp teeth of the T-Rex as it loomed over him. He quickly pulled his stone and cards from his pocket and swiped Chomp's card as fast as he could.

Just as Zoe predicted, Chomp transformed in a flash of light into a full-size, real-life Triceratops. This time he wasn't chasing the D-Team, however: he was protecting them! Chomp roared, lowered his horns, and charged towards the T-Rex like a prehistoric rhino. The Tyrannosaurus looked up and prepared to do battle with the Triceratops – and Max was safe for the moment! He scrambled to safety, and the D-Team and Dr. Taylor looked on as the two huge beasts approached each other.

With a snarl and a roar, the two dinosaurs smashed into each other and started fighting. It was a fearsome sight – two beasts the size of houses ripping at each other with their claws and trying to bite each other with their massive jaws. Chomp tried to spear the Tyrannosaurus with his long, sharp horns, but the T-Rex had killer teeth and was made for fighting. The D-Team watched nervously from a distance as Chomp wrestled with the prehistoric killer.

However hard he tried, though, Chomp just couldn't get the better of the T-Rex: it was just too big and strong for him. The Tyrannosaurus used its strong jaws to grab one of Chomp's horns, and before long it was clear that Chomp was losing the fight. 'What can we do?' wailed Zoe. 'Chomp is going to get beaten! We have to help!' There didn't seem much the D-Team could do to help – but Dr. Taylor had an idea. 'Try the second card, Max!' he cried. 'It might do something!'

Max pulled his cards out of his pocket – he had forgotten about the second card from the tree! What would it do? Could it bring another dinosaur to life? Or have a magic effect on Chomp? As the T-Rex let out a mighty roar and unleashed another ferocious attack on Chomp, Max grabbed the card and swiped it fast along the lightning symbol on his stone. The team held their breath. 'Is anything happening?' hissed Rex. 'Wait and see!' said Zoe. 'The stone is glowing, so it must do something!'

Suddenly, Chomp backed away from the Tyrannosaurus and started to glow and sparkle. It was as if a huge power was building up inside him – electrical power, spilling out as he moved along. He looked stronger, faster and meaner than he did a few seconds before. With sparks flying off him and a bright glow shining from his skin, he fixed the Tyrannosaurus in his sights. Then he charged again, FAST!

The dinosaurs smashed into each other once more, but this time Chomp was ten times stronger than the Tyrannosaurus. With a blinding flash, the T-Rex went flying through the air, and landed with an earth-shaking thud at the edge of the forest. Defeated, he changed back into a card, and the angry Alpha Gang ran back into their aircraft to escape. Chomp had won, thanks to his special battle move! 'Wow! Electric Charge was amazing!' said Max, reading the words on the move card that had saved the day.

Relieved, Max shrank Chomp back to normal again by swiping his card. The D-Team cheered – but Dr. Taylor was looking thoughtful. 'It looks like we aren't the only ones who know the secret of the dinosaurs!' he said, stroking his beard. 'We're going to have to be very careful from now on!' As Chomp nibbled on his trouser leg, Max agreed. They would need every bit of D-Team bravery to protect the dinosaurs from the strange Alpha Gang, whoever they were!

D-TEAM WORDSEARCH

Can you find all of these D-Team words in the grid below?

MAX

CHOMP

DR. TAYLOR

```
B T D T E A M P L B D
E H Y B M V C X F D R
K E B G S A P A T I T
U R R R N Z O C J X A
P O Z H N K L E V B Y
E B D O H X V I Y T L
W Y T M E D R C U L O
K U B R Y N E B G J R
F Q P E O N S G T Z F
I P A B Z O C H O M P
K A B G T P H Z I L H
T R Z A R C L J X S W
D I N W L D R V G Q L
T S C K B F R E M A X
```

ZOE

PARIS

REX

ACE

D-TEAM

21

ELEMENTS PUZZLE

The elements are a very important part of the dinosaur cards.
Draw the element that comes next in each row below!

FIND CHOMP!

Max is looking for Chomp everywhere.
Help him out by picking the path that leads to the right dinosaur!

DINOFILE: CHOMP

Find out about the D-Team's Triceratops!

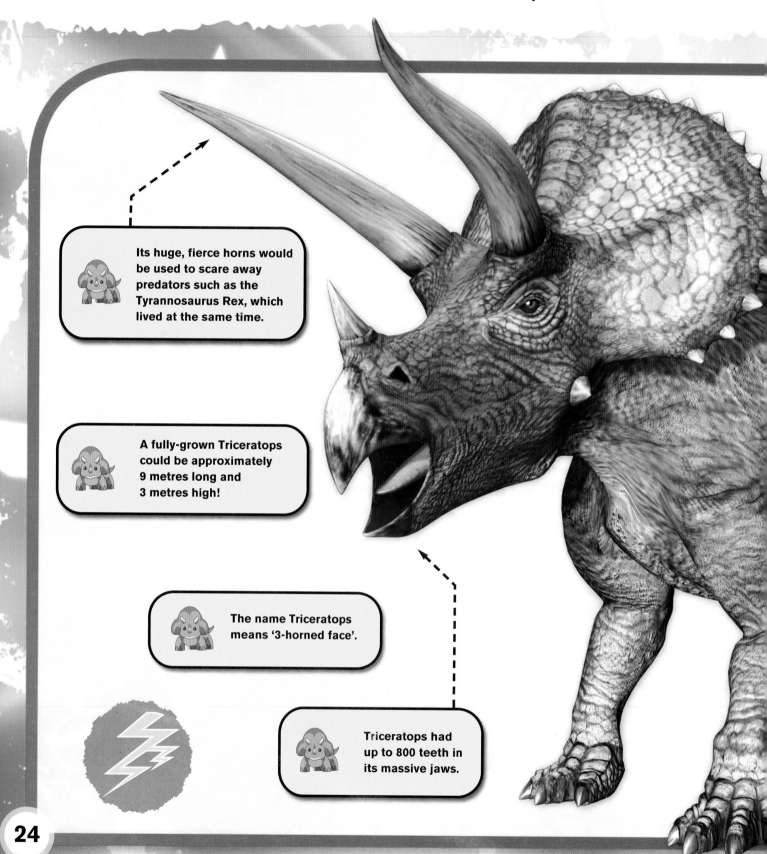

Its huge, fierce horns would be used to scare away predators such as the Tyrannosaurus Rex, which lived at the same time.

A fully-grown Triceratops could be approximately 9 metres long and 3 metres high!

The name Triceratops means '3-horned face'.

Triceratops had up to 800 teeth in its massive jaws.

KEY FACTS

Name: Chomp
Partner: Max
Type of dinosaur: Triceratops
Element: Lightning

Its skin was very thick and scaly!

Triceratops was a very fierce dinosaur, charging at its enemies like a modern-day rhinoceros.

Triceratops roamed the earth around 65 million years ago, making it one of the more 'recent' dinosaurs!

Despite its huge size, Triceratops only ate plants, not other animals.

TERRY COLOURING

Terry is ready to change into battle mode.
Lay on some colour to give him energy.

Terry is an angry red colour, but you can use your imagination to make your version any colour you like!

NAME THAT DINOSAUR!

Can you name the Dinosaur King dinosaurs
below just by looking at their shadows?

1.

2.

3.

4.

5.

6.

TRUE OR FALSE?

How much do you know about dinosaurs?
See if you can tell which of these facts is **TRUE** or **FALSE**.

1. The word dinosaur means 'terrible lizard'

TRUE ☐ **FALSE** ☐

2. The biggest dinosaurs were over 40 metres long

TRUE ☐ **FALSE** ☐

3. Tyrannosaurus Rex only ate plants

TRUE ☐ **FALSE** ☐

4. Dinosaurs were actually reptiles

TRUE ☐ **FALSE** ☐

5. Some dinosaurs had 5 feet

TRUE ☐ **FALSE** ☐

6. Dinosaurs are closely related to modern birds

TRUE ☐ **FALSE** ☐

7. Dinosaurs didn't have teeth

TRUE ☐ **FALSE** ☐

8. Dinosaurs hatched out of eggs

TRUE ☐ **FALSE** ☐

9. Dinosaurs died out around 5000 years ago

TRUE ☐ **FALSE** ☐

10. They were discovered by professor Dino Saur in 1930

TRUE ☐ **FALSE** ☐

THE MISSING PIECE

Terry and Chomp are in the middle of a battle!
Which of the three missing pieces completes the picture?

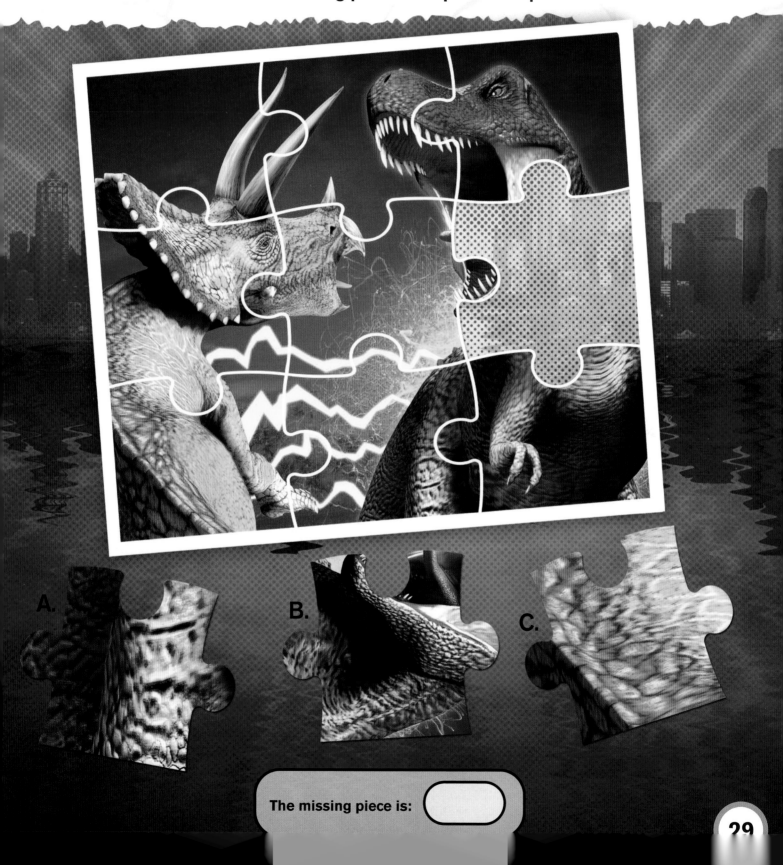

A.

B.

C.

The missing piece is:

DINOFILE: TERRY

Find out about the Alpha Gang's Tyrannosaurus Rex!

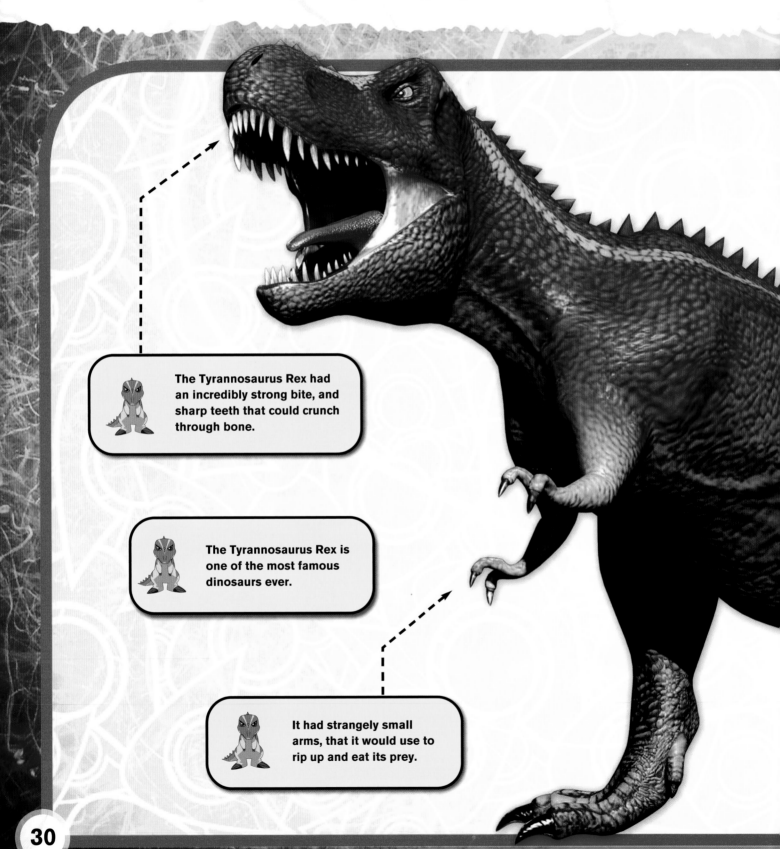

The Tyrannosaurus Rex had an incredibly strong bite, and sharp teeth that could crunch through bone.

The Tyrannosaurus Rex is one of the most famous dinosaurs ever.

It had strangely small arms, that it would use to rip up and eat its prey.

KEY FACTS

Name: Terry
Partner: Alpha Gang
Type of dinosaur: Tyrannosaurus Rex
Element: Fire

 It was a fierce predator, killing and eating other dinosaurs.

 It lived around 65 million years ago, around the same time as the Triceratops.

The name Tyrannosaurus Rex means 'Tyrant Lizard King'.

Its large, strong legs could carry it along at up to 25 mph.

FIND THE CARDS!

The D-Team are chasing down magic elements before the Alpha Gang arrive.
Follow the maze below, picking up the elements on the way!

START

FINISH

HIDDEN NAMES

Cross out the numbers in each row below
to reveal the names of these dinosaurs.

1. P3A45866R789A43
S543A34U34R3O54
3L5O435P5H54U5S

2. C543A657R8N4OT
253AU54R2U432S

3. S4P324IN432O43S
4A765U8R2U765S

4. S9876A34I2C23
H2A432N4I276A

DINOSAUR BATTLE

**Terry is in the middle of a ferocious dinosaur battle.
Draw in his opponent to complete the picture!**

Write the name of your dinosaur here:

DINOFILE: ACE

Find out about the D-Team's Carnotaurus!

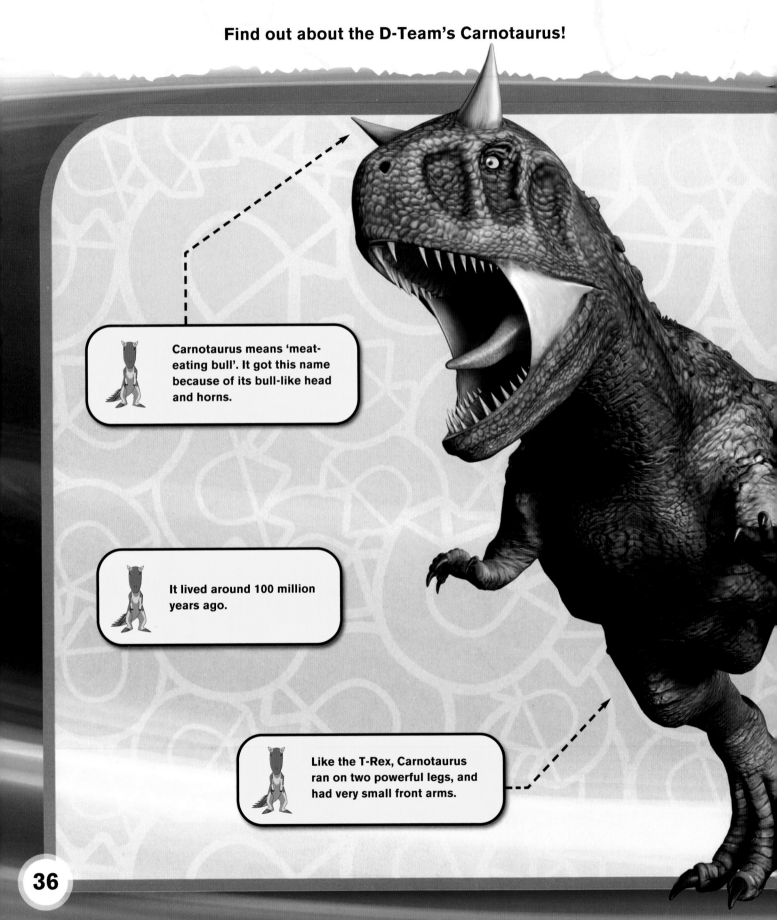

Carnotaurus means 'meat-eating bull'. It got this name because of its bull-like head and horns.

It lived around 100 million years ago.

Like the T-Rex, Carnotaurus ran on two powerful legs, and had very small front arms.

KEY FACTS

Name: Ace
Partner: Rex
Type of dinosaur: Carnotaurus
Element: Wind

Carnotaurus was a medium-sized dinosaur, and grew to approximately 8 metres long.

Carnotaurus had a long row of larger scales running along its spine, making it look more fierce.

A meat-eating predator, Carnotaurus was smaller than a T-Rex, but was still fierce enough to kill and eat smaller animals.

BATTLE FOR THE DINOSAURS

Play against a friend to find out who is the Dinosaur King!

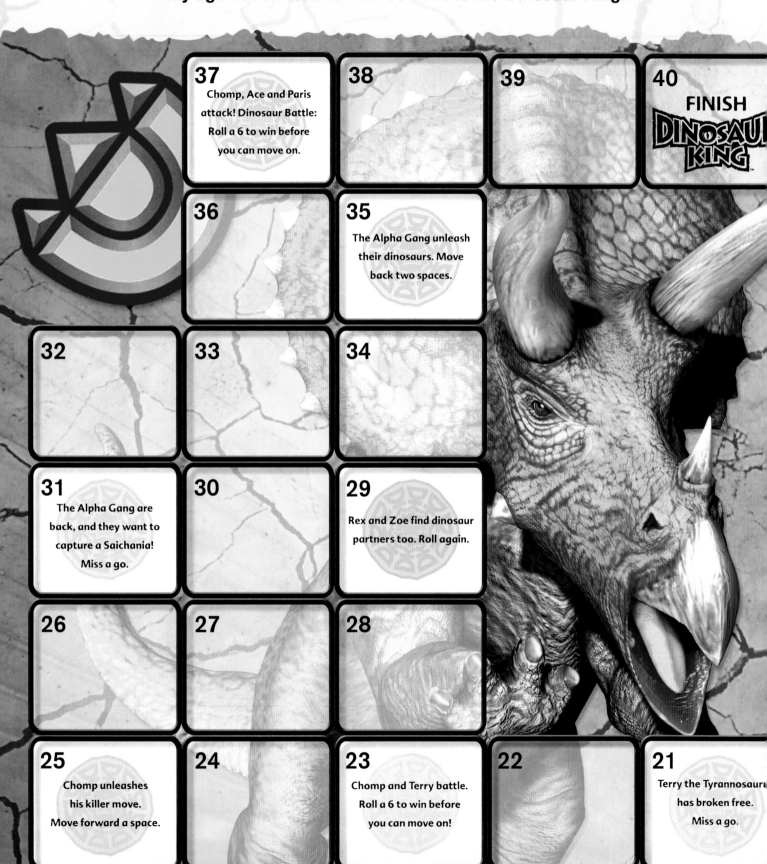

37 Chomp, Ace and Paris attack! Dinosaur Battle: Roll a 6 to win before you can move on.

38

39

40 FINISH DINOSAUR KING™

36

35 The Alpha Gang unleash their dinosaurs. Move back two spaces.

32

33

34

31 The Alpha Gang are back, and they want to capture a Saichania! Miss a go.

30

29 Rex and Zoe find dinosaur partners too. Roll again.

26

27

28

25 Chomp unleashes his killer move. Move forward a space.

24

23 Chomp and Terry battle. Roll a 6 to win before you can move on!

22

21 Terry the Tyrannosaur has broken free. Miss a go.

HOW TO PLAY

- Flip a coin to see who goes first
- Roll the die and move forwards the number of spaces shown
- Obey any instructions on the squares you land on
- First one to the finish line is the Dinosaur King!

START

2

3 You find a mysterious card in an old tree. Move forward three spaces.

4

5 You unleash a wild Triceratops! Miss a go!

8

7

6

9 Chomp becomes your own pet dinosaur. Roll again.

10

11 You learn to use your Dino Holder to control dinosaurs. Move on two spaces.

14

13

12

15 Another card has been discovered. Race on a space!

16

20

19 Dr. Z finds the card first. Go back three spaces.

18

17 The Alpha Gang are on your tail. Miss a go.

DINOFILE: PARIS

Find out about the D-Team's Parasaurolophus!

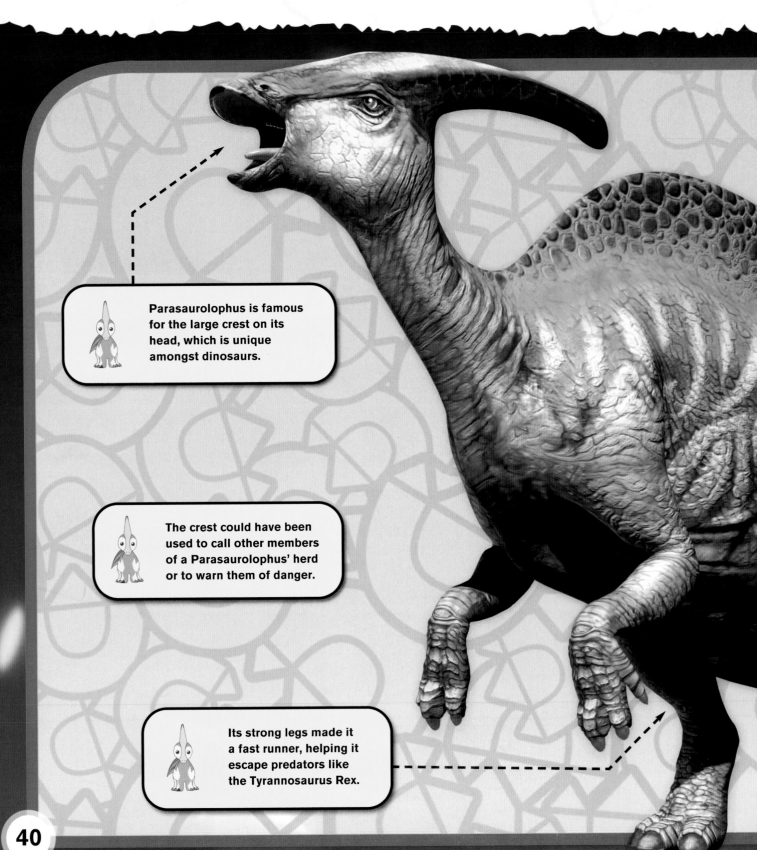

Parasaurolophus is famous for the large crest on its head, which is unique amongst dinosaurs.

The crest could have been used to call other members of a Parasaurolophus' herd or to warn them of danger.

Its strong legs made it a fast runner, helping it escape predators like the Tyrannosaurus Rex.

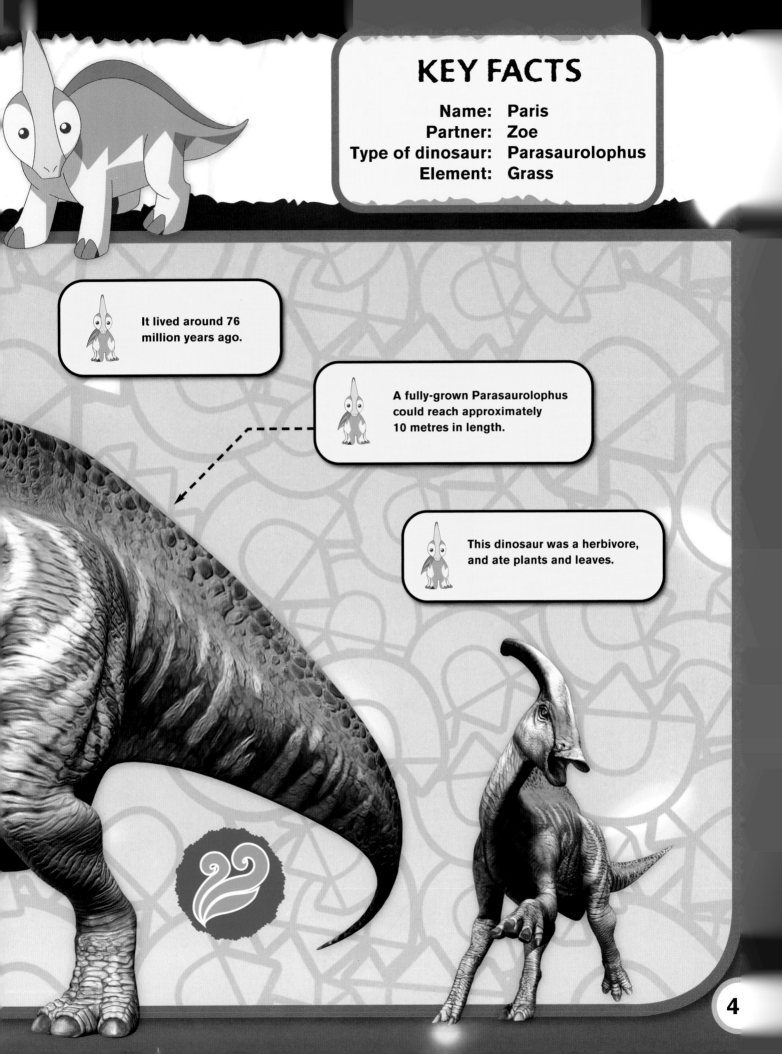

KEY FACTS

Name: Paris
Partner: Zoe
Type of dinosaur: Parasaurolophus
Element: Grass

It lived around 76 million years ago.

A fully-grown Parasaurolophus could reach approximately 10 metres in length.

This dinosaur was a herbivore, and ate plants and leaves.

BATTLE AT THE PYRAMIDS

It was mid-afternoon at Dr. Taylor's D-Lab, and the D-Team were puzzling over the new Dino Holders that Dr. Taylor had created to hold their mysterious stones. There were voices echoing out of the holders – hundreds of voices, all saying 'Help us! Help us!' Zoe scratched her head and listened closer. Could the voices be dinosaurs, calling them to help? 'It's possible!' said Dr. Taylor. 'The Dino Holders can translate the dinosaurs' thoughts into words, so that we can hear them!'

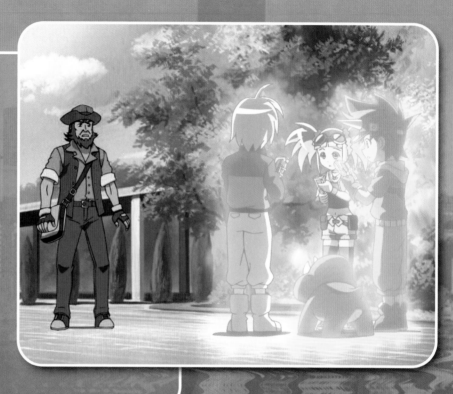

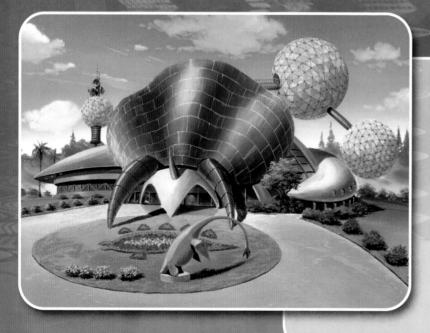

The team headed into Dr. Taylor's hi-tech lab to investigate further. 'Have you read the manuals for your D-Holders?' asked Dr. Drake as they walked in. The team groaned. 'But the manuals are huge!' moaned Rex. The voices were still coming from the Dino Holders, though. 'I think the Dinosaurs want us to protect them from the horrible Alpha Gang!' said Zoe. 'But how can we help? We don't know where they are!'

As Dr. Taylor was about to reply, he was interrupted by the telephone ringing. He answered the telephone and a video call popped up on the D-Lab's giant screen. Rex was surprised to see his father, Dr. Owen, looking down at him from the screen. 'Hello dad!' cried Rex, waving. 'What are you up to?' Dr. Taylor waved hello too. Dr. Owen was his dinosaur research partner, and he assumed he had made a dinosaur discovery of some kind!

The D-Team gathered round to watch, and Dr. Owen began to explain. He was on a dinosaur dig in Canada, and they were excavating a large set of ancient bones. But in amongst the usual dinosaur relics, his team had made an important discovery…they had dug up a set of small cards too. Dinosaur cards. 'I remember you were telling me about your recent adventures,' said Dr. Owen, 'and I thought these might be of interest to you!'

Dr. Owen held the cards up for the D-Team to see. Sure enough, they were just like the cards Max had found in the hollowed-out tree. Except instead of a Triceratops, the cards had two different dinosaurs on them: a Parasaurolophus and a Carnotaurus. The team looked at each other in amazement. 'That's two more dinosaurs we can bring back to life, just like the Triceratops!' cried Max, as Chomp ran round the D-Lab nibbling at everything he could find.

'Two new dinosaurs! Two new dinosaurs!' sang Zoe. 'That means we can have little dinosaur pets like Chomp!' As she hopped from foot to foot, Rex pleaded with Dr. Taylor. 'Can we keep them as pets, can we, please?' Dr. Taylor nodded. 'I don't see why not. It will be interesting to research!' he said, watching Chomp nibble at Max's foot. 'Dr. Owen, can you send us those two cards as fast as you can please?' he asked. Dr. Owen nodded. 'Of course!' he replied. 'I'll send them over express – you'll get them first thing tomorrow morning!'

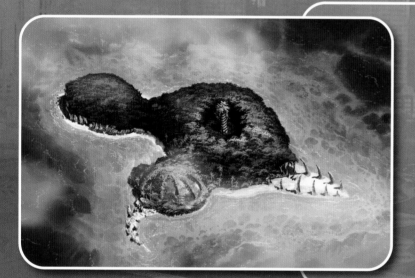

Meanwhile, on a remote island base, someone else was interested in the dinosaur cards that were popping up all over the world. Dr. Z and his Alpha Gang were looking for them too, from their hi-tech secret lair at Zeta Point – an island that could move through the water to avoid being detected by Dr. Z's many enemies. He had built a lab there to rival the D-Lab – but instead of studying dinosaurs, it was built to capture them!

In his lab, Dr. Z was pacing up and down and muttering to himself. 'I need more dinosaurs!' he grumbled. 'I've only got one, and I'll need dozens of them to stage the dinosaur battles that will make me rich, famous and powerful beyond my wildest dreams!' He strode up and down, waving his fist in the air. 'More dinosaurs! But where will I find them? I need a card to appear, or I'll never be the Dinosaur King!' he cried.

But Dr. Z didn't have to wait long. At that moment, in the Egyptian desert, a small egg broke open to reveal a dinosaur card. No-one was there to witness it, but the card fluttered away in the breeze. It had a picture of a Spinosaurus on the front, and a symbol for the element water. It fluttered across the desert, into a nearby town, and along a street, where the card landed on the floor of a café. When a passer-by spilled a drink on it, the water activated the card – and to everyone's shock, an enormous, full-size Spinosaurus erupted from the card and into the real world!

The massive dinosaur smashed out of the café and began to rampage down the narrow streets of the Egyptian town. People screamed and fled as it stomped over cars, smashing trees and signs out of its way and scattering crowds of people. What was this huge monster? Where had it come from? It looked just like a dinosaur, but surely they had died out millions of years ago! No-one knew what was going on!

Before long, news of the dinosaur smashing through the town spread across Egypt – and then across the world. News crews and TV cameras dashed to the scene, and broadcast images of the dinosaur on the news. Most people couldn't believe their eyes – but when Zoe flicked on her TV and saw the scene, she knew exactly what was going on. She grabbed the phone and rang Max straight away. 'Switch on your TV!' she cried down the phone. 'I think we've found another dinosaur!'

The D-Team rushed to the D-Lab, and Dr. Taylor called up a map of the world. Sure enough, a light was flashing in Egypt – it was a confirmed dinosaur appearance. The team grabbed their Dino Holders, which were flashing too. 'We have to get out there!' cried Max. 'The Alpha Gang are probably on their way right now!' Rex was jumping up and down with impatience. 'But how?' he said. 'That dinosaur is halfway across the world! And we don't have a private aeroplane, or spaceship, or whatever it is the Alpha Gang fly around in!'

Dr. Taylor grabbed the phone and started ringing travel companies. 'I need a flight to Egypt!' he cried down the phone. 'As soon as possible!' but Dr. Drake held her hand up to silence everyone. 'I have an idea!' she said. 'Technically, your Dino Holders are linked to the dinosaurs you are looking for!' she explained. 'Which means that it's just possible that you could use them to teleport yourselves to Egypt!' Max and the D-Team looked at their Dino Holders closely. 'Really?' said Rex. 'Is it safe?' but before Dr. Drake could answer, Max had jumped up and was ready to go. 'Send us to the desert then!' he cried, before vanishing into thin air!

When he re-appeared, he and Chomp were in the middle of a hot, dry desert, his Dino Holder glowing in his hand. 'Wow!' said Max, making sure he had no injuries. 'It worked!' He looked around at the miles of sand and pyramids, before groaning. 'Oh, no!' he said under his breath. 'Look who's beaten us to it!' Sure enough, there was the Alpha Gang, already in the desert and hunting for the rampaging dinosaur. And what's worse, they had brought their pet T-Rex with them!

Before Max could do anything, the Alpha Gang had unleashed Terry the Tyrannosaurus, who charged through the desert, snarling and roaring. Within seconds he had found the huge Spinosaurus – and Max looked on helplessly as the T-Rex engaged the other dinosaur in battle. Max gulped – he had seen Terry in action before, and it was a fearsome sight. He hoped the Spinosaurus was tough enough to see him off!

Terry was too strong for the new dinosaur, though. He reared up to his full height and smashed the Spinosaurus over, sending him crashing to the floor. Defeated, the Spinosaurus changed back into a card and fluttered down to the ground. Max watched as Ursula dashed over and picked it up. 'Yessss!' she cried. 'The Spinosaurus is ours! We've got double dinosaur power now, ha haa!' But Max had other ideas. 'Not so fast, old lady!' he said, grabbing his Dino Holder. He swiped Chomp's card and unleashed the Triceratops. 'You're not getting that Spinosaurus without a fight!' he cried as Chomp grew to his full, enormous size.

Chomp lowered his long horns and pawed at the sandy floor, before charging at Terry at full speed. 'Go Chomp!' cried Max as the dinosaurs crashed into each other once again. 'You can beat him! Use your horns!' The dinosaurs wrestled and struggled with each other, crashing into the ancient pyramids and sending huge lumps of stone flying. But Terry was still stronger than Chomp, and the Triceratops was soon struggling against the mighty Tyrannosaurus Rex.

Terry knocked Chomp over with a massive blow to the head, then dived in and used his killer jaws to crush Chomp's back with a devastating bite. Chomp roared out in pain, before staggering back and collapsing onto the ground. 'Chomp!' cried Max in horror, as he watched the Triceratops fall over. Terry smashed Chomp with blow after blow as he lay collapsed on the ground. 'Get up, Chomp!' cried Max, running over to the battling dinosaurs. But Chomp was unconscious.

As Max sprinted across the desert, however, he heard a shrieking voice behind him. 'Take that, you pesky boy!' cried Ursula, and Max wheeled round to see her swipe a dinosaur card of her own, with a blinding flash of light. Before his very eyes, the card grew and transformed into a huge, fierce dinosaur: it was the Spinosaurus the Alpha Gang had captured a few minutes ago – and Ursula was using it against him! Max gulped and staggered backwards.

'I'd like to see you fight two dinosaurs at once!' cried Ursula, as the Spinosaurus reared up and let out an ear-splitting roar. Max backed away from it slowly, looking up in terror at its rows of razor-sharp teeth. 'Chomp!' he wailed. 'Help! Quick!' but Chomp was still collapsed at the foot of a pyramid, and Terry was still rearing over him, hitting his limp body as it lay on the ground. Max stumbled and covered his eyes, as the Spinosaurus growled and moved in for the kill...

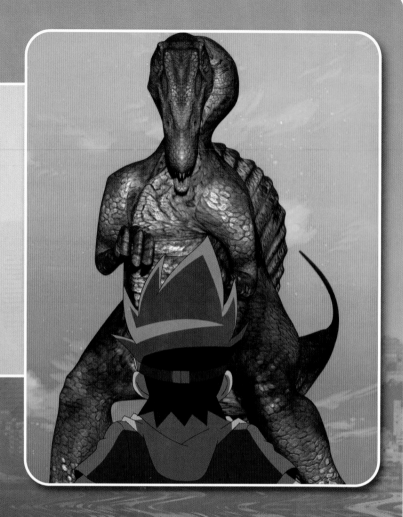

But three seconds later, Max still hadn't been eaten. He peered up through his fingers, and was amazed to see the Spinosaurus backing off, as if it was scared. 'What the...' said Max. 'Why is he running away?' A roar behind Max provided the answer. He looked over his shoulder in time to see a big, blue dinosaur galloping towards the Spinosaurus. Behind the dinosaur, Rex was waving his Dino Holder in the air. 'Meet my new pet!' cried Rex. 'Ace – attack!' Max grinned. 'Rex! Am I glad to see you!' he cried.

Rex's dinosaur, Ace, lowered his head and smashed into the retreating Spinosaurus. The dinosaurs tussled for a moment, but Ace was strong, and with a mighty butt of his head sent the Spinosaurus crashing to the ground. Defeated, it changed back into a card – which Ursula immediately swiped off the floor with a scowl. 'You kids just don't know when to stop!' she hissed. Meanwhile, another dinosaur had charged up and was standing next to Rex and Max. Zoe hadn't been left out – she had a brand new dinosaur, and she wanted to see it in action!

'Meet Paris!' cried Zoe, running up behind the Parasaurolophus. But Max didn't have time for introductions. He was rushing over to where Chomp was being pounded by Terry at the foot of the pyramid. 'Do something!' he wailed. 'Chomp is badly injured!' Zoe and Paris ran up behind him, and Zoe pulled out her Dino Holder. 'I think I have just the thing!' she said, pulling out a move card and swiping it quickly. 'Paris – use Nature's Blessing!' As she swiped the card, a green swirl of energy flowed out of Paris's body, and into the limp, injured Chomp.

As the blessing flowed from Paris into Chomp, the Triceratops slowly opened his eyes and looked around him. His whole body started to glow, and he slowly rose to his feet and blinked his eyes. It was as if he was waking from a dream – and he showed no signs of the injury Terry had dealt him moments earlier! 'Chomp!' cried Max, overjoyed. 'You've healed him!' Surprised, Terry backed off and watched as Chomp shook his body and reared up again, stronger than ever.

'Time to finish this off, I think!' cried Max, pulling a card out of his Dino Holder. 'Chomp – prepare for an Electric Charge!' He took the move card and swiped it through the holder. Chomp lowered his horns, and began to glow as the power of his special move built up inside his body. Sparks and lightning bolts zapped around him, and Terry stepped away, scared of the new strength his enemy had.

Chomp pawed the ground, then flew at Terry in a super-powered charge. The dinosaurs met with a roar and a bright flash, as Chomp's electric charge exploded into the Tyrannosaurus Rex. With an agonized roar, the T-Rex flew through the air and crashed, limp, onto the desert floor. 'Yessss!' cried Max, punching the air. 'You did it, Chomp! Way to go!' Terry's card fluttered to the ground, and an angry Ursula picked it up and added it to her Spinosaurus card.

Faced with the new, stronger D-Team, the Alpha Gang started to retreat slowly. Chomp, Paris and Ace were a fearsome sight as they roared and growled at their enemies, and Max and the D-Team giggled as the Alpha Gang stumbled out of their way. 'Run away!' cried Ursula, making a dash for their aeroplane. 'We'll be back!' she yelled over her shoulder as Chomp pawed the ground menacingly. 'And we've got Spiny the Spinosaurus to help us now, too!'

'It's true!' said Max as the Alpha Gang blasted into the sky and made their escape. 'They've won another dinosaur, which will make them even stronger!' But Rex was too excited to worry. 'Yes, but we've got an extra two dinosaurs to help us fight them!' he said, pointing at Ace. 'And I've got a new pet Carnotaurus to play with!' The D-Team giggled as their small dinosaur pets ran around the desert nibbling at their legs.

'And I've got one too!' grinned Zoe, petting Paris on the head. 'And she's the cutest dinosaur ever!' But Max was still worried. 'Well, we'll need all of their special powers if we're going to see off Dr. Z and his Alpha Gang!' he said, as the D-Team trooped across the desert towards a pyramid. 'Now how about we do some sightseeing while we're over here in Egypt? I think we've earned ourselves a holiday!' But they all knew that it wouldn't be long before they had to face the evil Dr. Z once more...

DINOFILE: SPINY

Find out about the Alpha Gang's Spinosaurus!

KEY FACTS

Name: Spiny
Partner: Alpha Gang
Type of dinosaur: Spinosaurus
Element: Water

 Spinosaurus gets its name from the scary-looking 'sail' that juts out from its back. No-one knows what it was for, but it looks mean!

 Spinosaurus was even bigger than a T-Rex, making it the largest meat-eating dinosaur.

 A fearsome predator, the Spinosaurus would rip its prey apart with its crocodile-like jaws and razor-sharp teeth.

 Spinosaurus lived between 144 and 99 million years ago.

D-TEAM IN ACTION

Can you spot the 6 differences between these two pictures of the D-Team?

ALPHA GANG ATTACK

Can you find all of the Alpha Gang
words below hidden in the grid?

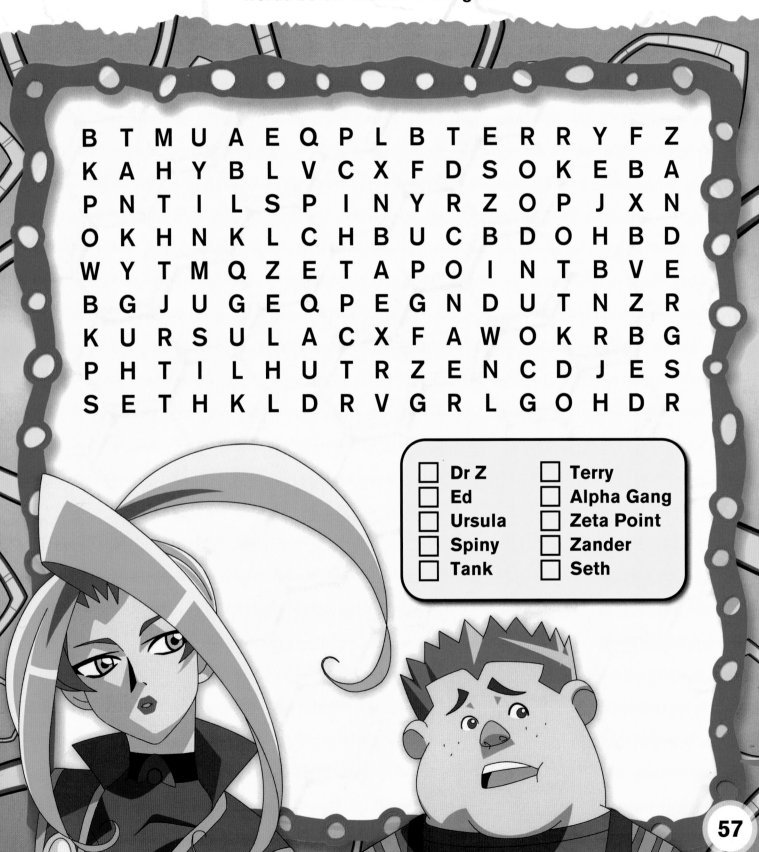

```
B T M U A E Q P L B T E R R Y F Z
K A H Y B L V C X F D S O K E B A
P N T I L S P I N Y R Z O P J X N
O K H N K L C H B U C B D O H B D
W Y T M Q Z E T A P O I N T B V E
B G J U G E Q P E G N D U T N Z R
K U R S U L A C X F A W O K R B G
P H T I L H U T R Z E N C D J E S
S E T H K L D R V G R L G O H D R
```

- [ ] Dr Z
- [ ] Ed
- [ ] Ursula
- [ ] Spiny
- [ ] Tank
- [ ] Terry
- [ ] Alpha Gang
- [ ] Zeta Point
- [ ] Zander
- [ ] Seth

WHICH D-TEAM MEMBER ARE YOU?

Answer the questions below to find out!

1 HOW LONG HAVE YOU BEEN INTERESTED IN DINOSAURS?

A) Since you learned about them at school.
B) For ever. You were born liking them!
C) For a year or two.

2 HOW DO YOU LIKE TO RESEARCH DINOSAURS?

A) You read books about them when you get home.
B) Your friends tell you stuff about them.
C) You watch programmes about them on TV.

3 HOW OFTEN DO YOU FIND YOURSELF IN TROUBLE?

A) Not often – only when your friends get you into it!
B) All the time, but it's not your fault!
C) Only when you say something you shouldn't…

4 IF YOUR COMPUTER BREAKS DOWN, CAN YOU FIX IT?

A) Yes, every time.
B) No, you haven't got the patience.
C) You can normally figure out how, but it takes you a while.

5 WHICH ONE OF THESE DINOSAURS DO YOU LIKE BEST?

A) Carnotaurus
B) Triceratops
C) Parasaurolophus

6 WHEN YOU'RE FACED WITH A PROBLEM, HOW DO YOU LIKE TO SOLVE IT?

A) Use your knowledge to find a logical solution.
B) Jump in and try something, quick!
C) Think about it patiently then choose the best solution.

7 WHAT WOULD YOUR FRIENDS SAY YOUR BIGGEST FAULT IS?

A) Impatience
B) Always getting in trouble.
C) You don't have any faults, you're perfect!

8 WHAT'S YOUR SENSE OF HUMOUR LIKE?

A) You like a clever joke about dinosaurs.
B) You'll laugh at anything!
C) You love it when other people do stupid stuff.

9 OUTSIDE OF DINOSAURS, WHAT IS YOUR MAIN HOBBY?

A) Computers.
B) What do you mean, outside of dinosaurs?
C) Fashion and music.

10 IF YOU HAD YOUR OWN D-TEAM, WHAT ROLE WOULD YOU PLAY IN IT?

A) The brainy one.
B) Leader, of course!
C) The one who always gets things done.

HOW DID YOU DO?

MOSTLY As

You're just like REX

You're clever, level-headed, and like to take things at your own pace. You can get impatient with other people if they don't keep up with you, plus you're great with computers and technology!

MOSTLY Bs

You're just like MAX

You're a natural leader and you love getting stuck in to whatever you are doing. However, you're not very patient, and your natural curiosity can get you into trouble!

MOSTLY Cs

You're just like ZOE

You're calm in a crisis, don't panic when you're in trouble, and can always think of a solution, whatever the problem. Plus you're into fashion and hanging out with your friends, as well as dinosaurs of course!

DINOFILE: TANK

Find out about the Alpha Gang's Saichania!

KEY FACTS

Name: **Tank**
Partner: **Alpha Gang**
Type of dinosaur: **Saichania**
Element: **Earth**

 It also had a club-like tail to help it defend itself.

 Saichania's back was covered in tough armour and spikes to protect it from predators.

 To help it cope in the desert, Saichania had a salt gland in its nose to help it find water.

 Saichania lived in the desert, and had an extra tough mouth, to help it eat rough, spiky plants.

Page 21   D-TEAM WORDSEARCH

```
B T D T E A M P L B D
E H Y B M V C X F D R
K E B G S A P A T I T
U R R R N Z O C J X A
P O Z H N K L E V B Y
E B D O H X V I Y T L
W Y T M E D R C U L O
K U B R Y N E B G J R
F Q P E O N S G T Z F
I P A B Z O C H O M P
K A B G T P H Z I L H
T R Z A R C L J X S W
D I N W L D R V G Q L
T S C K B F R E M A X
```

ANSWERS

Page 22   ELEMENTS PUZZLE

1. EARTH. 2. GRASS. 3. WIND. 4. EARTH. 5. FIRE.

Page 23   FIND CHOMP!

PATH B

Page 27   NAME THAT DINOSAUR

1. ACE. 2. PARIS. 3. SPINY. 4. TERRY. 5. CHOMP. 6. TANK.

Page 28   TRUE OR FALSE?

1. TRUE; 2. TRUE; 3. FALSE; 4. TRUE; 5. FALSE; 6. TRUE;
7. FALSE; 8. TRUE; 9. FALSE; 10. FALSE

Page 29   THE MISSING PIECE

THE MISSING PIECE IS B.

Page 32-33   FIND THE CARDS!

FIND THE CARDS!
The D-Team are chasing down magic elements before the Alpha Gang arrive.
Follow the maze below, picking up the elements on the way!

START

FINISH

Page 34   HIDDEN NAMES

1. PARASAUROLOPHUS; 2. CARNOTAURUS;
3. SPINOSAURUS; 4. SAICHANIA

Page 56   D-TEAM IN ACTION

Page 57   ALPHA GANG ATTACK

```
B T M U A E Q P L B T E R R Y F Z
K A H Y B L V C X F D S O K E B A
P N T I L S P I N Y R Z O P J X N
O K H N K L C H B U C B D O H B D
W Y T M Q Z E T A P O I N T B V E
B G J U G E Q P E G N D U T N Z R
K U R S U L A C X F A W O K R B G
P H T I L H U T R Z E N C D J E S
S E T H K L D R V G R L G O H D R
```

Josks
books